Princess Not so Charming

BY ARIELLE HANA LACKRITZ

Front cover image by SenpaiDesign
Book desgn by SenpaiDesign

ISBN: 978 - 1 - 7357107 - 0 - 9

Printed and Published by Kindle Direct Publishing

First Printing edition 2020

Dedication

To my editor who puts up with my
many ideas and is always there as my sound board
when I get stuck.
Love you!

Tremaine

Charming

Ferrand

White

Swan

Lourant

Chapter 1

Once upon a time there were five small kingdoms that lived in harmony with one another and lived happily ever after... Ha! Yeah right. Five kingdoms living in peace with no conflict or political unrest what a load of bull.

Sure the princess of the White kingdom was able to snuff out the politically crooked Queen with the help of her seven small protectors and even found love; and of course the little unappreciated squire boy was able to pull a magic sword out of a stone, becoming the new king. Not to mention the story of my late mother Queen Ella, better known in stories as Cinderella, finding escape from her wicked step family by falling madly in love with my father, now retired king of the Charming Kingdom. However my mother died several years ago, and King Arthur's peaceful reign did not last as long as everybody had hoped it would.

Let's start from the beginning shall we, well the beginning of my story; my name is Princess Alexis Charming of the Charming Kingdom. I am the daughter of my late mother Queen Ella, who died after 12 short years of happiness with my father and our blooming family. My father although saddened by losing her takes great pride in my brother and lives for how much my appearance reminds him of my mother. My brother now holds the title of King Charming, with his wife Lillian at his side, and has two children on the way. I on the other hand...

"Princess Alexis!" My maid Sophie, calls for me from the balcony above.

I stand below in a knights training uniform, my hood up so nobody recognises me; although my stature is getting harder to disguise as I grow older. Sophie looks down to me and I point towards the garden to throw her off course. I turn to see a tall familiar figure topped with his unmistakable ash brown hair walking towards the training grounds, I run to fall in beside him, giving him a small push. "Morning Xander." I greet cheerily.

Xander and I have known one another since we were small, his father was a general in our kingdom, Xander would always come along to the palace and we would play and later train together. Xander has followed in his footsteps and is in line to take over his father's position. We have been inseparable since the moment we met, I was never one to get along with other girls, I don't tend to have the same hobbies.

He quickly regains his footing. "Where did you find the knights training armor this time Alexis?" Xander simpers; but has more a look of disapproval and amusement.

"Knight John really needs to keep better track of his belongings."

Xander chuckles, "I will remind him to do so. Do you really think it is a good idea to practice today?"

"Just let me get a little bit of practice in before turning me in."

He sighs, "You really shouldn't do sword training, it's not proper for a princess-"

"Yeah, you know that spiel doesn't work on me right?"

He chuckles, "Yeah well I promised your father that I would at least try."

I smile excitedly, "Besides, today is archery training, I promise not to touch a sword today."

We turn and are nearly to the armory next to the training grounds when I see my father speaking to one of his advisors; I swiftly square my shoulders and pull my hood lower as we walk past him. I'm about to grab a bow when I hear his voice, "Alexis, what have I told you about doing unladylike activities?"

I sigh and turn to see he is giving me a stern look. "Why can't I practice both? A woman should be able to protect herself if need be."

He raises a brow, "In what scenario would you need to take up a bow and arrow or a sword? You are nearly joined at the hip to Xander and he is talented enough to keep you safe if need be."

I look to Xander who is smiling pridefully whilst readying to join the others at the archery range. I cannot conjure an answer so he continues, "Alexis you've grown into a beautiful young woman...just like your mother." He gives a watery smile and I avert my eyes. He clears his throat, "Sophie is looking for you to fit you to your gown for tonight."

"Tonight?" I look back to Xander who is trying to sneak away from the conversation. Coward.

"We are having the annual ball tonight, remember? I expect you to be there." I start to say something but he cuts me off, "It's not a suitors ball, you know that we marry for love in this kingdom. However you never know who you might meet at a ball, that is how I met your mother. Now go return the armor to its rightful owner and stop worrying Miss Sophie. The stress you have caused that poor woman over the years is nearly visible on her face."

I sigh and trudge back to my room.

"Tried to go train this morning dear sister?"

I scowl as my brother Tybalt, who joins me in the walk back to my room. "I don't understand why he won't let me train and study the same things as you."

"It is custom for a princess to act as a lady." He states as if reading it from a book on royal etiquette.

I let out an aggravated sigh, "But I know how to act the part of a princess as well."

4

Tybalt immediately barks out in laughter, and I realize I chose the wrong moment to itch the inside of my nose.

"What? I can if I choose to."

He gives me a look like he begs to differ, "You may know etiquette, but your execution is far from what our family name would suggest."

I roll my eyes, "I still don't know why I need to learn it, it's not as if it will help me speak politics; it only teaches me to be quiet which I find quite uncomfortable."

"Just try to humor father, the ball is a tradition, and from what I hear he has chosen a very special dress for you to wear tonight."

I give him a curious look as he smiles and walks away. I've never liked any event that requires me to wear a dress, I feel weighed down and stiff, as well as too vulnerable and weak. Heels are not a footwear I deem pleasant and makes it harder to sneak or run away if need be.

When I open the door to my room I see my mother's blue dress on the bust. I reach to hold the piece of glass charmed on the chain I wear around my neck and unease settles in.

"There you are! Why are you in those masculine clothes again?" Marian scolds from behind me. Although Marian is but a cousin, she is more like a much older sister to me. She is the epitome of being a royal lady and though we are quite close, she has never approved of my hobbies or choices in style. She was engaged once, however her fiance, Erec Ferrand First Prince of the Ferrand Kingdom, was massacred along with the rest of the Ferrand family; the Tremaine's now rule their land and it is now known as the Tremaine Kingdom.

I always enjoyed when I saw Marian and Erec together, he even saved me from a wild dog when I ventured too far in the woods chasing Xander when we were young children. I was 9 when word of Tremaine's take over and the massacre of the Ferrand family had happened; I had to help Marian through such difficult times, she was devastated and some of the light in her eyes had dimmed that day.

A few ladies come in helping me out of my training gear and into the dress. They get it ready for altering and send me to get my makeup and hair done. I grumble as they poke and prod me with their hellish tools.

"So are there any prospects on the horizon?" Marian asks slyly.

I roll my eyes, "Only the one that matters."

Marian grins, "Have you two talked about it?"

I give a gentle smile back, "No we don't speak of it, we act as we always do and I'm absolutely fine with the way things are now. There is no rush."

I don't think I've ever seen such an ugly face on my cousin before, she looks displeased with my answer. "You two are perfect for one another, I don't understand at all what you both are waiting for."

"I don't think he is ready, Xander still wants to rise through the ranks by merit and wants to be sure it would not be due to connections; he wishes to prove himself."

Her face transitions to sorrow and her eyes filled with longing, "You know, you don't know what the future holds Alexis. You need to grasp on tightly to what's important to you before you lose it or it's taken away from you."

I look to my cousin and know that the wisdom she has given me is the truth and something to live by.

The ladies finish with my hair and makeup, I notice that once again they have ignored my wishes and have covered up the scar striking through my right brow. It is a small battle scar from training with Xander, but I like to wear it with pride. Knowing I'm not going to get my way I quickly stand with my cousin who has shaken herself out of her funk and has started to impart the latest gossip of all the kingdoms, such as King and Queen White are trying for a baby. I mostly tune it out; smiling and giving her automated responses. "He is looking for a queen to rule with him; he is to take over the kingdom from his father in the coming months. It would seem he has his sights set on someone; I guess we will find out tonight at the ball."

I had moved to the washroom for privacy, although in reality I am polishing my sword that I hide behind the large chest of linens near the bath. I look up from polishing, "Wait. Who is looking for a queen?" I ask, most of the older kings have already transitioned their thrones to an heir of their choosing, although there are some outside our treaty that have sons old enough to take the crown, but my father usually doesn't invite those outside the treaty to this ball.

She gives an annoyed exhale, probably knowing I haven't been listening, "First Prince of the Tremaine Kingdom, Damian Tremaine."

"Is someone hoping to get chosen?"

"A few ladies of court in all the kingdoms have been vying for his attentions, for the last few years actually."

I see my disgusted look in the mirror opposite me, "Marian...are you interested in Damian?"

"Absolutely not; why would you even ask such a thing."

She sounds as disgusted as I look. "It was his father that did such horrible things so long ago; and you more than anyone should understand a child being nothing like their parent. Maybe Damian is different than his father." Marian's mother was not the nicest when speaking of ladies of court, it was why Marian chose to visit so often and how we ended up being such great friends.

"I suppose you are correct, however I would never go near that family nonetheless. Besides that boy is too young for an old spinster like me."

I laugh, "You are still young cousin and I wish you to find happiness soon."

"You still have to wonder how all those ladies of court fawn over him, knowing full well how his father came to sit on the throne."

Damian Tremaine, many would call him exceedingly handsome, he has short obsidian hair that frames his face, strong features, and sapphires for eyes. Although from what I've heard of his kingdom his family could only be described as criminals. His people are grossly over taxed and he mistreats his staff; not to mention the grueling training of his soldiers. Not many ladies of court pay attention to the politics of men, I however don't trust a single gender to know what is best for an entire species, especially one that plays in the tacit political jungle we find ourselves in.

"Your dress is ready and it's almost time for the ball. We should finish getting ready." Marian says breaking me from my thoughts.

My shoulders immediately slump forward and I hide my sword and polishing kit.

Once I have the dress on once again it fits me perfectly. When I look in the mirror, the women in the room are tearing up. "You look so much like your mother."

As I stare at my reflection I can't help but disagree. Sure I'm wearing her dress and have similar features such as my light, almost white, blonde hair, and the blue in the dress brings out my matching blue eyes; however, I feel awkward and out of place within her dress and my chest feels as if it is tightening.

My father is announced and let into the room, his eyes alight with happiness; my family's happiness is my weakness so I gather all the grace I can muster and greet my father with a tight lipped smile and he leads me down to the ballroom.

Chapter 2

The ball is in full swing and I am hiding behind the buffet table with a small plate loaded with horderves, looking like a puffy blue cream puff with my skirts nearly swallowing me. I hear a stern voice clearing his throat and look up to see my father smirking and shaking his head in disapproval although his eyes glint with amusement. I roll my eyes and stand, placing my plate on the table and taking his outstretched hand.

He takes a glance at the plate before turning us to walk towards the dance floor, "Were you really planning on eating all of that?"

"It was the plan but apparently my corset won't allow it." I pout.

My father chuckles as we take position to join others in dancing, this seems to be the only day he finds my lack of charm amusing. This ball is held on the anniversary of when my father King Charming met my mother Ella.

"Thank you for wearing her dress tonight. I felt that since you are of the same age she was it would only be right for you to wear it." I look up into my father's eyes and see how much joy my likeness brings him. "You remind me of her, you know? Not just the way you look, but your actions as well."

I arch a brow, not believing his words and he laughs; "I remember mother as graceful and more ladylike then myself."

His eyes alight with nostalgia, "She was, but she also spoke her mind and didn't like to conform to the royal life I provided for her." He sighs and shakes his head, "She was always helping the cooks and maids around the castle; always disguising herself so she could go about the garden without staff treating her differently."

I give a small smile, "I didn't know about those things. She always seemed so adamant that I learned the ways of being a lady of court."

"Yes, well you might not have recognised her when she dressed that way. I also believe that she was only trying to impose her inability to act like royalty and wished for you to be able to fit in. I know you don't like that you must learn to act as a lady, but please know it is only so-"

"Excuse me Lord Charming, may I cut in?" We both turn to see Prince Tremaine.

My father smiles and places my hand in his, "But of course Prince Tremaine." My father turns to kiss my cheek and whispers in my ear, "Be nice."

I simper at my father before turning to bow to the prince as he bows to me and we start to dance.

"May I say although you are always beautiful, tonight you are gorgeous."

I shake my head and plaster on the fake smile I've been taught to give, "And you look very respectable tonight Prince Tremaine."

His eyes wander to my neck and a slight chill runs down my spine at his leering. "May I ask about the glass shard you wear around your neck? I couldn't help but notice every member of your family wears a shard as well."

"Very perceptive of you. Have you heard the story of how my father and mother found one another."

He looks at the shard, "It is a piece of the slipper she wore?"

I nod. "My family wears it as a reminder that we do not care of ones background and that as long as the difficult path you take leads to something worthwhile, all is meant to be."

"I've heard much of your mother and I have to say that I admire that she didn't come from a royal lineage. Those who are able to rise in the ranks of society are to be revered."

"Yes she is infamous and held in high renown. I hope to make her proud one day."

"You have already achieved what you seek;" he says forwardly, "I hear much about you as well Princess."

"Really? Like what?"

"That you are as beautiful and kind as your mother Queen Ella, nearly the spitting image."

"The only thing I hear is that I'm not as charming as my name would suggest; although I have to say I take more pride in that description."

"I'm sure your beauty and renown far exceeds the need for charm... you seem to be the only woman I notice at gatherings such as this. I have to say that I do hope you may accept me as a future husband." I can't help the confusion that I know transfigures my face. "It would seem that even my people speak highly of you and I believe that if I take you as my wife it will raise their opinion of me as well. My people are not fond of the way my father took over the kingdom, it would seem that King Arthur Ferrand was quite popular before my father killed him and assumed the throne."

"You speak so callously of such a tragedy." I say trying to mask my distaste for his tone.

"Yes well he wasn't taking his position seriously and his son would only fall in his footsteps." He says matter of factly and unapologetically. "I plan to take full advantage of the gift that will be passed down to me from my father. I only need a wife that can placate the citizens while I do what needs to be done; I have no doubts in my mind that you will be my bride and we will rule the Tremaine Kingdom together."

My head jerks back in nonbelief that someone would ever assume that I would follow such an idiotic notion. "I do apologize but our family is well known for marrying for love and not politics, so my answer is no. Although I am but a princess, I'm well aware of what your family does to its people and their opinion of you. If you think they will quiet their grievances because I marry you, your thoughts are misguided."

He squeezes my hand roughly and his tone turns harsh. "The candor of your charm was no exageration; but believe me when I tell you that your so-called kingdom needs me as an ally and I don't take slanderous comments lightly even from princesses. I can and will make things very uncomfortable for your kingdom and family, so take a few days to think about my proposal. You seem like a smart woman Alexis, and I believe a glance into the trade routes within the kingdom will change your mind. Also your disbelief in marrying you calming the citizens, well that tactic seemed to work well for your father wouldn't you agree?" He lets go of me roughly and bows, "It was a pleasure dancing with you princess." He plasters on a smile that doesn't meet his eyes and makes my skin crawl as he leaves to speak with other guests.

What the hell did that mean?

"Are you alright Princess Alexis?" I turn to Xander who is bowing. His hair has been cut so that it is shorter on the sides and longer on top, leaving enough hair to be pull back and tied with twine. His hazel eyes look more green tonight, they seem to fluctuate between a browner hazel all the way to almost green with a hint of navy creeping in from the outside of the iris. His eyes always fascinated me.

"Yes I'm fine, but I believe I'm quite done with this party already." I shake the sour mood Damien had left in me and then beam up at Xander. "Would you mind helping me sneak out?"

He shakes his head, a grin cracks the stern look he had and softens his features. "I really believe you should stay."

"And why is that?" I ask coyly.

He grabs my hand gently, twirls me into his arms, and starts to dance. "Because I haven't been able to dance with my best friend and princess at a party since last year and I can't miss the opportunity to do so when you look so beautiful in your mother's dress."

I shake my head and give a tight lipped smile, Xander tilts his head trying to regain eye contact and my smile morphs into a mischievous one. "Okay one dance and you'll help me escape?"

He laughs and whispers flirtatiously in my ear, "I'll even spar with you after Princess." Xander twirls me a few times and we settle into a swaying rhythm.

"Do you not like wearing your mother's dress?" He asks.

I sigh and look away from him, "I feel uncomfortable wearing it."

"How so?"

"Don't misunderstand. I love that it was my mother's dress, but I don't feel like myself and that makes me feel more distant from her."

"Although you don't agree with your likeness to your mother, I have to say I disagree. I remember

Queen Ella as kind and loving, and you embody that everyday." He lifts my chin so I am looking at him, "However if you still feel uncomfortable then you must fashion the dress so you feel more comfortable next time you wear it," he says confidently.

I shake my head no, "I can't ruin such a beautiful gown my father loves so dearly."

His eyes dim in sorrow hating he can't make me feel better but I beam up at him when I realise the music is fading to an end, "Song is over Xander, now let's get out of here."

"I'll meet you at the training grounds, I must go change as well." He says laughing and leads me out of the party.

*   *   *

"So are we going to talk about what Prince Tremaine said to ruffle you?"

I strike at Xander and he blocks, "He gave me research to do."

"What kind of research?" he asks as he counters.

I parry and then step back lowering my sword; Xander lowers his as well, "Something he thinks will make me want to accept an offer he made to me." Concern immediately transforms his face but I wave it off, "I'd rather not speak of it until I have all the facts. Do you think you can keep my father and brother away from the library tomorrow morning."

Xander smiles, "I will try my best Princess."

Chapter 3

I jolt out of bed when I am woken by the first birds starting to sing songs. It is still dark outside but I hurry to put on a robe and sneak to the library; Prince Tremaine's musing and threat last night bothers me. When I have a stack of books that I believe to be relevant on one of the tables I pull out a map and spread it out on the desk.

As a princess I was not taught much about politics, but that didn't stop me from sneaking into the library to learn. Trade within the kingdoms was one topic that my brother and father went over a lot over the years so I never had much access, thankfully it would seem they returned most of the missing books back to the library, so I won't need to go sneaking into the office to steal them.

As I read I find that all trade goes through what is now known as the Tremaine Kingdom and his is the only kingdom that borders with the rest of the continent. I also find that the next kingdom is situated farther away, it would seem there are a large number of villages and forts in between his castle and the bordering countries castle. Although each of our five kingdoms is on the smaller side individually, other countries know of our treaty; if anyone moves on one of our kingdoms the others within the treaty will join in arms to protect the land being threatened. I put down the book I'm reading and go in search of several trade logs and a few books on our neighboring kingdoms.

There are five kingdoms and we all have a peace treaty that was forged several generations ago by the original families that had claimed this land. The treaty is one of peace and to unite our kingdoms during times of foreign threat. However if there is a civil squirmish it is to be dealt with by the respective kingdom; we do not intrude on other kingdom affairs unless asked.

I find the resources I'm looking for and come back to find a cup of tea set out on my desk, when I look around I see no one in sight. I smile when I recognise the cup as part of the set my brother's wife uses almost exclusively. Tybalt was crowned reigning king only a few months ago, so he still relies heavily on my father's opinions and wisdom. His wife, now known as Queen Lillian, is quiet and kind; however I've heard her speak sternly with him before, she was one of the few ladies of court I had respect for. Although she doesn't dabble in politics, Lillian is very smart; with her new found royal standing she has followed in my mother's footsteps, trying to better our citizens' livelihoods and education. I sip the tea and open my new books.

What I find is very troubling and the realization of what Prince Tremaine said being true only makes me feel more cornered by the second. My stomach churns with every new realization.

The Tremaine family is ambitious and power hungry. Seeing as they are the middleman for trade between foriegn countries and our kingdoms, this means they could potentially have more allies outside the treaty that we within the five kingdoms are unaware of, which makes the Tremaine Kingdom far stronger.

Damian had also said something about my father marrying my mother to placate the citizens, I wonder what he meant? I turn to the library trying to think of what references I would need to answer my questions.

"Hiding in the library today? I thought for sure the missing princess would be hiding amongst the new recruits leaving for survival training today." my father asks, startling me as he approaches my desk, I look out the window noticing how sunny it is, it must be close to noon, he looks at the books on my desk. "Why the sudden urge to read about the affairs of state and trade routes?" He looks up at me with a smile and a raised brow, "Interesting combination."

"They were finally available to read and I thought I would look at them while you and brother weren't using them." It is the truth, I did want to look at them even before Prince Tremaine had said anything. "Father..." I almost don't want to hear the answer I know I'm about to receive, so much so I don't want to ask the question preceding it.

"Yes?"

"Why do we rely so heavily on the Tremaine Kingdom?"

He looks rather confused by my question, "We rely on King Tremaine's kingdom the same as the other kingdoms."

I look down at the desk truly horrified that no one has ever noticed what I now know is true; I step away from the desk and start to exit the library. How can nobody see it? Although it's true that all the kingdoms rely on one another; it would seem that no one has noticed that the Tremaine Kingdom has made itself the sole primary merchant to all the kingdoms. My guess would be that the Ferrand family would never take advantage of their true power and no one questioned that power when the Tremaine's took over.

"Why the sudden interest in this topic?" My father asks before I can even pass him.

"I've decided to accept a marriage proposal that was given to me last night."

The sound of glass shattering turns my gaze. My father stares at me in shock; I glance and see he dropped his cup of tea.

"Oh? Who?"

"Prince Tremaine." I state flatly, not allowing emotion to cross my face or voice. "I thought I would read up on my fiance and his kingdom before accepting."

"Damian?" My father asks, clearly confused. "I wasn't aware that you knew him well."

I stay silent.

"You love him?" My father asks, I can see the skepticism in his eyes.

"Is there a problem in choosing him? From what I can see marrying him will be very advantageous."

"No your choice is not a problem as long as you're happy." My father says warmly.

I nod and kiss his cheek as I try as steadily as possible to exit the library. When I walk into my chambers the seamstress from the day before is laying out an outfit for me.

She bows, "Princess Alexis, I've just finished a tunic that was commissioned for you." I walk over and see the garment; the seamstress leaves, bowing once more as she exits. The garment is the same blue and styled bodice of my mother's dress I had worn last night, but the sleeves and bottom hemline reminds me of the tunic I wear for archery. I slowly put the tunic on and retrieve some trousers from my secret stash of mens clothing. The bodice is easy to lace together myself and fits perfectly. I stand and stare at my reflection, finally seeing the resemblance to my mother as well as being extremely comfortable.

I grab a bow and some arrows from their respective hiding place behind my wardrobe and head to the archery practice grounds.

My chest and throat are tight and my stomach is in knots. I feel...need. The need to release my anger and frustration, the need to fix...something... The need to scream.

21

I feel..I feel.rage.

I've been told all my life by the men around me that learning politics and how to weild a weapon would be of no use to a lady. With what I've learned I truly would love to stick each of their heads in a full chamber pot, at least their words would be in a rightful place. Now as all women, I am left to pay for man's ignorance and those blinded by complacency. I must now marry a man who I do not love, a man I know to be cruel to his own people and with no prospects to change his ways. I wish to grab a sword and have a few rounds with a dummy, but instead I raise my bow and an arrow; I am less likely to be seen and stopped out here where a large shed can shield sight of me. I slow my breath and let all of my emotions fly with the arrow I let go. My mind then goes blank and it is just my weapon and the target, I no longer exist; just nothing but the target, the bow, and the arrow.

I don't know how long I've been practicing before I feel Xander's presence, all I know is that the sun has started to descend, "Thank you so much for the tunic. You have no idea how much it means to me." My voice is shaking and I don't know if it is because of my anger or that I feel like I'm about to break down crying.

Xander stays silent and I know he has heard the news. He takes my hand, making me lower the weapon in my hold, and looks at my fingers that I had not noticed are bleeding, his face nearly crumpling when I refuse his seeking gaze. "You must stop before they fall off princess." He says as he wraps a clean cloth around my hand.

"It would seem I don't have a choice." I balk as I briefly meet his gaze, I can not look him in the eye; I can see pain behind his strained warrior face, however his eyes are distorted with frustration and unhappiness. "He holds more power than any of the other kingdoms realise, including my own father and brother."

Silence.

I wrap my arms around him, burying my face in his chest.

"Are you sure there is no other way?"

I shake my head with a shudder, I don't think I've cried since my mother's passing when I was young; but my eyes burn and I let two tears break free when he encases me in his arms, only two; one for rage and frustration still encased in my chest and one for what I am being forced to leave behind... my cousin was right, we waited too long.

Chapter 4

I leave for the Tremaine Kingdom today. My family and the other kingdoms are to join the wedding in a few days. Xander is waiting near the carriage, his face as stone carved as my own.

My brother and Lillian await at the castle entrance. "Safe travels dear sister." My brother's face looks uneasy.

"Thank you brother, may I ask for a going away present?"

He looks at me curiously, "I'm unsure of what I can conjure in just a few minutes before your departure, but I can be sure to bring it with me to the wedding."

I shake my head, "I only ask that you research what I have laid out on your desk; and try to keep your findings from father. He doesn't need to know what you find."

He tilts his head not understanding but Lillian speaks up, "I'll be sure he studies what you have left out for him."

Lillian's eyes meet mine and I see true understanding in them. I nod and turn to walk over to my father who waits next to the carriage as well.

"I feel compelled to tell you that if you ever change your mind before the wedding, you can come back, no one will think less of you."

"I'll see you at the wedding in a few weeks father." I give him a kiss on the cheek and he smiles before stepping away to join my brother and sister in law at the entrance.

I turn to face Xander, "You don't have to come to the wedding if you don't want to but please make sure my brother fixes what we spoke about."

Xander nods, "I still wish you would let me escort you to the border."

I shake my head, "Trust me it is hard enough leaving you here; but do promise me two things. Plus I already have four guards coming on what should be a quiet journey."

"Anything."

"Write often...and find happiness."

His jaw ticks, "I can definitely do one of those things." He leans in and whispers, "But my happiness is dependent on your presence in my life."

I turn my head and grimace; Xander opens the door of the carriage and helps me inside.

I refuse to look back as we begin our short journey to the Tremaine Kingdom.

*   *   *

We have entered the Tremaine Kingdom and are to arrive at the castle later tonight. My carriage comes to a stop and I hear the clang of swords. "Princess, please stay in the carriage," calls one of my guards. The sounds of swords continue and I a few arrows lodge in the door of the carriage. I roll my eyes, stand to untie my skirt, and exit the carriage. I grab a sword from an unconscious soldier and stand armed just as my last guard falls. The trip was to be a short peaceful one and I see that we are largely outnumbered.

"May I ask why you have chosen to attack my entourage?" I ask in mock boredom and annoyance. I'm surrounded by armed men wearing masks and take to a defensive stance.

"We are bandits, some may call us the merry men of the dark forest."

I look around taking in the squabble that had ensued before my exiting the carriage, my men are unconscious but still breathing. "Merry indeed, you throw quite the party boys." I answer in mock impress.

One of them approaches me closer, "We happen to notice your carriage at the border. We've heard news of your wedding princess and any ally of the Tremaine family is our enemy."

"You stand against the Tremaine family?" A bit of hope rises within me.

"We wish to make their lives as difficult as possible, save the people of the land, and to thwart their future plans by any means necessary." Says another who comes from behind me, he stands with a sword pointed to my face, but I smile and stand unflinching. He shuffles his shoulders slightly, "You are no ordinary princess."

"Thank you. I choose to take that as a compliment."

I can see his posture falter and take my chance; quickly I toss my arm knocking the sword away from myself as a target, I then raise my sword to his throat. His hood falls but he wears a face covering; his eyes are that of a heathered green meadow. I feel as if I have seen similar eyes before, the man raises his hands in surrender and a crescent shaped scar on his left hand catches my eye. I look at the man again, my head cocked in confusion and recognition. "You saved me when I was little." His eye brow ticks as if he is trying to hide something and seems uncomfortable with my recognising him.

I step back, eyes full of excitement, and swiftly drop my sword to the ground, "Take me hostage." I command. "I would like to speak with your leader. It would seem we may be able to benefit one another."

The man I had unarmed sighs, "And how could a mere princess be of any use to us?"

"I know how to sneak around, fight and wield weapons, and I have a grievance with the Tremaine family." I state bluntly. "Are there any other requirements for joining your band of merry men? I have to say although I have very strong views on gender equality, merry men roles off the tongue nicely so I won't even push for you to change the name."

"But you are a lady and a royal one at that." Interjects a man leaning against a tree, he wears a mask covering his eyes and amusement plays on his face. He is very tall and from what I can tell is the oldest man here.

"Perceptive of you sir," I say, and then quickly unsheath my hidden dagger and throw it, aiming at the tree close to the man's head. His eyes go wide in shock and I give the man a big toothy grin with a curtsy, I am a lady after all. "As you will all learn, most know me as the princess who doesn't live up to the Charming name. Even if you reject me, I will work against the Tremaine family."

"You may call me Robin." Says the man I had recognised.

I think back to my kingdom, knowing full well that I will have to change my name as he did, I smile because I'm known for stealing armor from Xander's friend, who has always been similar in stature to myself. "If we are using false names, you may call me John."

Robin smiles, "We already have a John among us, how about Little John?"

I hold out my hand, "Deal."

He goes to shake my hand but stops, "There is one other requirement to joining us and it is a difficult task to undertake." Sorrow and some regret swims in his eyes, but I wait for him to tell me this requirement.

"Are you willing to die for our cause?"

I take a moment, "Yes."

"You are willing to leave your family and loved ones behind causing them unnecessary pain?"

I glare up at him, "I choose to die today, however I also aim to return when the Tremaine family has been dethroned; and you will come back with me."

He looks me in the eye and I challenge him by keeping eye contact while taking his unwilling hand to shake on it.

Chapter 5

I now go by Little John amongst my bandit friends, although Robin and our oldest member Louvel still have a bad habit of using my real name at times.

Over the last four years we have been able to make the lives of the commoners of the Tremaine Kingdom bearable. We try our best to return some of the taxes back to the people; as well as break out or save those unjustly arrested. Our attempts at helping have become more difficult this last year, even our spy within the castle is having trouble helping us these days. The last time we went out to get back one of the larger tax collections, Damian set fire to the bursars' home with the whole family inside; I still wake up at night in a cold sweat because I was in town returning the money when it happened, I was forced to watch with the rest of the village. I would have been able to help if Damian and his guards left right away, but they stayed until the fire burned out. That was about a month ago, since then we haven't heard word of what Damian will be doing next; we believe he is about to make his move on his larger scale plans to expand his territory soon; but when?

Seeing how my death affected my family hurt, but the defeat I saw in Xander nearly broke my resolve. I see his hands tremble every time he reaches for the pouch I had gifted him for his knighting ceremony years ago, it's a small leather pouch that hangs from a cord around his neck; I had attached a charm of a shield onto it as well.

My resolve in staying dead to those outside Robin and his merry men redoubled after hearing that Damian's heinous plans go beyond what I had found in my research, my determination to disgrace Damian Tremaine became unwavering.

I do however sneak back into the Charming Kingdom to check up on my family and Xander a few times a year.

"Hey why are you hiding in a tree today?" I look down to see my niece and nephew looking up to the branch I'm perched on.

I jump down and smile. "This is my favorite tree."

"Why? It doesn't look any different than the rest." My nephew Alex asks, my brother had named him after me and my niece Ella is named after our mother.

I notice the necklace my niece wears, "That's a very pretty necklace."

She looks down, "Do you want it?"

I shake my head, "Don't offer me something so precious. Do you know the story behind this necklace?"

"No, I found it in an old jewelry box."

I then regale them with the story of the glass she wears.

"You come to tell us stories that others won't tell. How do you know so much?" my nephew asks.

"I used to live here." I say with a pained smile.

"Why do you not live here anymore?" My niece asks with curious eyes.

I sigh but smirk at how inquisitive they are, I look from side to side play acting that I am making sure no one is around to hear me and then whisper to them. "I'm on a secret mission." Their eyes bulge adorably as they look at one another and then back to me; I put a finger to my lips, "That's why you need to keep our story times a secret, I'm supposed to be working; if anyone finds out that I'm telling you stories I'll get in big trouble." They nod diligently, "Now can you do me a favor?"

They both smile and agree, so I send them back with a letter, reminding them to not say who it's from or that they saw me today. I watch as little Ella and Alex scamper up to Xander who is teaching some new recruits. He smiles down at them and accepts the letter; I then turn and disappear into the trees. One day I'll come back.

I have visited my niece and nephew many times but started telling them stories my last few visits; the stories are ones that I know will be hard for my family to tell, stories about my mother and I've told them about myself from an outsider's perspective as well. I feel partially responsible for what I had witnessed today, my niece and nephew snuck away from Sophie and went to the training grounds, that's how they found me.

*   *   *

It doesn't take long to get from kingdom to kingdom on horseback, however I feel safer once I make it back to the dark forest that I have called home for the last four years. True to its name the forest is filled with dark wood trees and impossibly dark green foliage; however the light mist that trails the ground makes the darkness mysterious and beautiful. My admiration of my home these last several years is interrupted as Louvel falls in next to me. "We had to move camp again."

"Where did we move to this time?"

"Down river, north of the cliffs."

"Wow we switched to the forest on the other side of the road?" I question as I turn back towards the road that I had just come from, giving my horse a small kick to go faster. Louvel follows suit.

"Went to spy on your family again? You know Robin doesn't like when you do that."

"First of all, he technically does the same thing, and second, he seems less angry if I have good intel to bring back."

"Information about your male suitor doesn't count as intel."

I give him a humored smirk, "He's competing, looks like he was able to change his guard schedule in order to compete. How is that for intel?"

"So are we going to enter the upcoming tournament?"

I smile mischievously and he laughs in response. Louvel is probably the tallest man I've ever met and he has shoulder length golden locks that frame a stubbled face and tired grey eyes, although he is the oldest of our group, his respect towards Robin is steadfast and he seems to enjoy us younger folk; he exudes pride in our rapscallion attitudes in our given plights. Louvel grounds us, imparting wisdom and aid to all those who seek it. "Wait, aren't you supposed to be distracting Robin from noticing my absence?"

"Yeah about that..."

"I asked him to fetch you." Robin calls to us as we dismount and tie our horses. My shoulders go up and I wince when I hear him. I look to Louvel who was meant to cover for me and he grins as Robin appears on my other side I kick Louvel in the shin and he toples over. "I asked him to bring you back to camp." Robin states bluntly. "Do you know how much trouble you could have caused if you had gone to our old camp, while the Tremaine knights were scouting?"

I roll my eyes and start to walk over to the fire.

"I know you like to check up on your kingdom, but it is too dangerous Alexis. What if you are seen?"

"I was only sizing up the competition for the upcoming festival." I say offhandedly.

"And what makes you think I'm letting you compete?"

I turn to stare in challenge, "If you are entering, I am as well."

"Really?"

"Yes Princess Alexis Charming is just as recognizable as Er-"

He cuts me off by clearing his throat and glaring at me; I notice the men surrounding us shooting curious looks our way, it still amazes me that these men don't know who he is, I counter with a knowing smile and Robin shakes his head, "If you are to compete, we must make sure you will not be seen no matter what."

"Robin! Sir!" A young man who has recently joined us is calling out in distress. He tries to catch his breath. "Sir, there is news that King Damian may be making his move on the citizens."

"When?" I ask my demeanor turning stern.

"He plans to make his move after the festival."

"Why after? The fact that he waits and has made no moves on expanding his territory has always confused me." Louvel queries.

"He needs his citizens present at the festival and citizens talk, he is the one to host the tournament this year. If he would've made a move before now, he wouldn't have citizens to attend and the other kingdoms would find out that he is breaking the treaty." I state bluntly. I have become more knowing of how Damian's mind works over the years. We have known about his ambitions to expand his kingdom since before I joined, I later came to the conclusion his end goal is to take the other four kingdoms in the treaty as well once he has grown his power in the bordering country. "I believe my death slowed his plans down. With the kingdoms bugging him to find a queen meant that he was under watch. As we all know he remedied that problem a little over a year ago."

My years of disguising myself in the Charming Kingdom have paid off, I sneak into Damian's palace often to look into what he has researched or signed most recently.

"Has your brother made any progress on creating a new trade route?"

I nod, "It would seem that he found the resources and is about half way done with construction on the port."

"How did you find out about the port he is building? If Damian were to find out, he may take drastic measures on the Charming family."

"He is being careful. The only reason I found out about it is because I was looking for the plans. Even if anyone saw the construction, they would only see citizens setting up docks for fishing."

Robin nods and turns to talk to all in the camp. "The festival is tomorrow, only a select few of us will go and compete; the reward for winning some of the challenges will help us get ready for our next plan, we must be sure to place at least two or three of the competitions." Robin shifts his gaze to me, "Neither you nor I are to win first place. First place winners are to show their faces to accept favor and our faces are not to be seen. Do I make myself clear?"

I nod, "Louvel and I will enter the archery competition, having two in that competition will better our chances."

Robin nods, "I'll be shooting for second or third place in the joust and I'll select a few to enter the fighting competitions as well."

Chapter 6

"Remember to keep your face obscured Alexis." Robin says as he lifts my hood to look me in the eye and then lowers it.

I smile at him and then lift my face mask, "Don't forget to keep your helmet on Sir Robin." He glares at me for my tart tone, before securing his helmet.

Louvel and I step out of the tree line and into the crowd; I always love the tournaments, my brother and Xander used to help me sneak off so I could change into commoners clothing and blend in so I could enjoy the festivities. As we pass one of the game stalls I stop when I see a hand sewn doll that reminds me of the one Xander had won for me. I place a few coppers on the stall and win the doll easily. "Congratulations on your win."

I nod and thank the man.

Louvel grabs my arm and pulls me through the crowd, "We are not supposed to make stops and play games here."

I put the doll inside the pouch at my side, "I am grateful their family still makes them, I very much enjoyed mine when I was a child."

Louvel gives a small smile and leads us to the sign up board. Louvel signs his name and hands the quil to me, I smirk and write.

"Why would you choose to write Robin?"

"Yeah, I can't put John this time, it would be too obvious to some in attendance and if our leader chose such a fine name I don't think he would mind if I borrowed it."

Louvel nods in agreement and we walk over to the jousting tournament where we find fierce competition. Robin could have won but he fixed to win third place and I watch as Robin claims his winnings and makes his way to the tree line, one of our own placed second as well and follows after Robin.

Calls for the archery tournament come next and we take our place amongst those who have signed up. We begin with the targets at 10 yards, and many last until 30 yards. Our completion however drops like flies as we near the 50 yard marks. I can tell all that there are still in the competition are knights from each kingdom and of course Louvel and I still stand as well. At the 60 yard mark we are grouped so only the best move onto the next marks.

"You are a very good commoner." There are only four of us left at the 80 yard mark, and I would know that voice anywhere. "Robin isn't it? Would you mind if I asked which kingdom you hail from and why they have not hired you to join their ranks?"

"We hail from the Tremaine Kingdom milord and I do apologise to the good knight, but my companion is not able to speak." Louvel says quickly.

"Is that right? Is there a reason he also hides his face?"

Louvel, always thinking on his feet, "Robin cannot speak due to the scarring on his face and he wishes not to scare the women and children."

"Is this correct Robin?"

I nod and keep my eyeline low, I have no misconceptions that he would recognize any part of my face.

The other man in our final group misses the target and Louvel goes next hitting the third ring. I know this distance is child play for Xandar so I aim for the second ring. Xander lets out a huff of laughter, "A man of your skill should not get second place just because you fear your face being seen." I see a mischievous smile quirk his lips from below my hood. He wouldn't.

Xandar takes aim and his arrow lands just outside the third ring, taking third place. My heart stills in my chest and I look to see the fear in Louvel's face. We are led to the Charming dias and each of us bow; Xander and Louvel step away and take their winnings and I am left standing before the ones who I once called my family. I feel my hands and knees shake, but they still when I hear my brother's voice. He sounds tired. "Robin you are unknown to our kingdom but you bested even our best archer and therefore have won first prize. Will you be accepting favor from my queen?"

I need to think fast. It's then that I see my niece and nephew. I shake my head no.

"No? Do you wish to insult my family young man?"

"Your Majesty he does not wish to insult you he just-"

I raise my hand to stop him and point at my niece. I then look up so slightly so only she can see my eyes; she beams and jumps down into my arms.

"It's you. The lady that tells us stories." she whispers quietly. And I raise a finger to my lips so she knows to keep it a secret. My nephew comes running, so I crouch down putting Ella on her feet.

Quietly I whisper for only them to hear, "Will you grant me a token of favor young one?"

She nods and plucks the blue ribbon from her hair and hands it to me with a big smile, "This will look pretty in your hair."

I fish the doll I had won out of my pouch, giving it to her. She jumps in excitement, "I know they don't let you run around the tournament so this is a thank you for keeping my visits a secret, I'll bring Alex something on my next visit," I whisper before standing and bowing down to them.

"Ella, that was quite dangerous dear and Alex, you know better than to run off like that." I hear Lillian scold.

"Just like her aunt isn't she?" My father's voice comes from my left as he drops my winnings into my hand. I bow and make for a hasty retreat while my Father gives his closing words for the archery tournament with parting words to all who had competed.

"That was very dangerous." Louvel scolds as we briskly make our way to where we are to meet Robin and the others.

"He purposely missed the shot, how was I to know he would do such a thing?"

"Robin is going to be cross with you."

"Why would he be cross with himself?" Calls out my father's voice.

Louvel and I freeze.

"I would think that anybody would be happy to win such a prize." Xanders voice chimes in.

"I hear you hide your face due to scarring; that should be no reason not to show your true skill in tournament young man."

I pull my hood further down.

"Young man I believe I also heard you mumbling to Princess Ella earlier as well." Xander states. "I thought you were mute?"

I stop Louvel before he concocts another lie for us to keep up with. "I do apologize Your Majesty. I wanted to compete in the tournament," I state in my altered voice which is definitely one of a woman but it is higher, shaky, and that of an older woman. Women are not supposed to enter such tournaments, "My goal was only to compete. My caretaker Robin let me compete as long as I didn't win and kept my identity safe. I do apologize most profusely Your Majesty, I meant no disrespect." I kneel to the ground to show my apology and the respect that should be shown to royalty.

"You are a woman." My father states blatantly. "You are rather good."

"Thank you, Your Majesty. It is also why I refused favor from Queen Lillian, I did not feel it proper. Your princess is quite adorable and I will cherish the token she has given me." I hold up the blue ribbon she gave me and then hold it to my chest.

"I was hoping you might be willing to work as a trainer in my palace." My brother's voice chimes in from behind me; I feel myself stiffen further. "You will not be able to fight or have knighthood, but no one in our castle will discriminate against a lady such as yourself to train our new recruits."

Shock fills me. Not having a problem with a woman training new recruits? That's new. I turn to face him and bow, "I appreciate the offer King Charming, but I will have to refuse. Now if you will excuse us, I have a scolding to attend." I turn and lead Louvel into the tree line, my family lets out a small chuckle as we leave. I smile thankful that my comment brought them even a moment of amusement.

*   *   *

"That was too close Alexis!" Robin shouts.

Why does he only use my real name when he is angry with me? "For the last time call me Little John and I won't apologize when my competitor purposely lost, I even only aimed for the second ring."

"Then you should have aimed for the third." He growls.

"I knew the archer, he had the ability to hit dead center and chose to miss!"

"Do you even understand what danger your presence being in our group brings! I let you in because I knew your motives and resolve to see everything through was as visible as mine was when I made my decision to band these men together. But revealing that you are alive would've led to the kingdoms finding our group and all that we have sacrificed over the years would have been for nothing! Not to mention what would happen with Tremaine and his plans!"

I hate being yelled at, it makes me feel as if I'm a child again or of all the times I had been scolded for not being ladylike nor having the hobbies of one. I grind my teeth, I know what Robin says is true and that I deserve hearing the words that he is shouting at me. When he stops screaming, he paces back and forth, his anger seething. "I apologize for my actions today, I will take whatever punishment you deem fit for any mistakes I made today." I state calmly.

Robin stops and is about to say something but two of our men burst into the tent. "Robin! We have spotted a spy." Says one of them, "what shall we do?"

Robin runs his hands over his face and then through his hair in frustration. "Bring him to the cliffs, if he has nothing good to say we can throw him off."

"Yes sir." They say in unison and then exit the tent.

Robin lets out a slow steady breath, "Little John, I know you didn't mean to win today, but that is no excuse when you think about the repercussions."

I look him in the eye, "I know."

"He and your family offered you a job at their castle, do you think they suspect?"

I shake my head no, "They think I am nothing more than a woman with some skill. They would have said something if they suspected it was me."

Robin nods, "I'm sorry to do this, but your punishment is that you are not to visit them until I say otherwise."

I nod diligently trying to suppress the hurt that is already gathering within myself.

"Now cover up so we can go greet our unwelcome guest."

"Yes Robin."

Chapter 7

"I told you I was only following an archer my king wishes to hire!" I hear from the cliffs.

I pull on my hood to hide my tied hair and begin to run.

"Little John what's the rush?!" Robin calls from behind. I hear him pick up speed to catch up with me.

When I get to the shadow of the tree line, I climb up the larger tree and perch myself on a branch; making sure to also change my voice into the higher shaky one that I used earlier, "What have we caught tonight boys?!" Xander looks up from where the men have him kneeling on the ground.

"A spy by the looks of it." Robin says from below.

"I am no spy sir."

"Only those who are bandits live in these dark woods. If you are not one of us, then you are a spy."

"Bandits?" Xander questions in anger and I can see a bright fire alight in his eyes, "Would you be the same bandits that killed Princess Charming four years ago?"

Everyone stands in silence and my shoulders stiffen.

"We may be bandits but we do not hurt women and children sir." Robin says breaking the silence.

Xander's face contorts into darkness, while his eyes flare with anger. "My name is Xander Nikolaidis, a knight of the Charming Kingdom; and I will have your heads for taking someone so irreplaceable from myself and the kingdom I am sworn to protect."

Robin turns to look up to me and whispers, "We need to be rid of him, he can't have knowledge of our group and where we reside. I know he is a knight from your kingdom, but we cannot allow him to leave here alive."

"He knows nothing that Tremaine doesn't know." I argue.

"But he is not from the Tremaine Kingdom, and from the looks of it if we let him go we will be hiding from two kingdoms. Tremaine will have no qualms letting another deal with us." Louvel chimes in.

Robin nods to him and looks back up to me, "He is only one knight, I cannot risk our animinity again today."

"I know you don't know who he is and I may be pushing my luck, but you have forced my hand." I jump from the low branch I had found perch on, turning my back to Xander. I glare at Robin and say the words that each man in our band of thieves can only udder once to make one final decision. "Over my dead body."

Louvel's eyes widen and so do Robin's. Robin searches my eyes, "Although I can not go against you after using those words; I do wish for you to be very careful with what you do with him."

"I use it for pardoning him, just as you would if she were to stumble upon our camp." I whisper.

Robin gives a sorrowful but understanding smile, "What we do with this one is up to you, however if he causes any problems I will be sure to kill him myself."

"Don't turn away from me you scoundrels! How dare you ignore me!" Xander shouts.

I nod to Robin in understanding and then turn to face Xander. "He may be rough around the edges Sir Xander, but I can assure you our leader is no scoundrel." I wave my hand and the men let Xander go, he stands.

"Anyone who lurks in the shadows and robs a young woman such as my best friend of her life is lower than a scoundrel; I am only unable to conjure a different word that is more fitting at this moment."

"Like my leader has said, we do not kill women or children much less men. We only take life if we are trying to save our own or innocents."

Xander widens his stance ready to fight, he clearly is not willing to listen.

"Would she be a woman to pick up a sword and fight by chance?"

Xander's jaw ticks. "Yes she would."

"I believe almost all present remember the young woman you speak of, myself included."

"If you remember her, you would know what happened to her." I can hear the resolve in his voice and see the glossy defeat in his eyes.

"If I tell you what became of this woman, do you swear on your oath as a knight that you will not speak of what you saw or heard on this night?"

"As long as it was none of you who ended her life then yes you have my word."

"Hmmm... that won't work actually." Xander looks at me confused. "Would we have your word if we let you have a fight with the one who ended her life?"

Rage pulsates off of Xander as he looks around at the men surrounding him, "I swear on my oath as a knight that I will not speak of what I heard or found here if I can duel with the one who killed Princess Alexis."

I smirk, "Perfectly stated...Now, give the man a sword!" I shout as I walk over to Louvel. "Do you mind if I borrow your sword?"

Louvel hands me his weapon and Robin takes hold of my arm, "Be careful with what you do."

"Do not worry Robin, he needs to release the anger that he holds before learning the truth." Robin looks at me skeptically, "He takes his oath very seriously, he will say nothing of what he sees or hears tonight." I promise and then turn back to Xandar.

I turn to see Xander take his sword from one of our men, "Who is my opponent?!" He demands.

I smile and step forward, swinging my sword in a circle before taking a defensive stance. "That would be me. I'm your opponent."

Xander takes an offensive stance, "By taking Princess Alexis's life you have rendered yours void; I must warn you that I will not hold back, nor think twice taking your life just because you are a woman."

"Good." I respond resolutely.

Xander attacks first and the steel of our blades crack like lightning in the silence, the force of his blow is stronger than I remember. However training with a large man such as Louvel has made me much stronger, I quickly counter with an attack of my own going for his weak spot and he surprises me with a block and then I feel the thin slice of his blade graze my arm. I back away quickly taking a moment to ready for his next attack, which comes swiftly from above and I block with a strike from below, our swords clash and stay in place as we use our force to try and gain the upperhand. It is in this struggle that I realize the tears that are coating the rims Xander's eyes; and as I take in my realization Xander knocks the sword out of my hand, kicks me to the ground, and then places the point of his sword to my throat. "I am not a man who takes pleasure in taking a life, much less a woman. However, I will make an exception in your case. Now, I must see the face of the one who took someone so precious from me."

"I do apologize profusely for the pain you have suffered Sir Xander." I use my normal voice as

I reach for my mask; Xander's blade tremors a bit. I take off my mask but leave my hood that still hides me.

Xander reaffirms the position of his blade. "You will never know the pain you caused by taking her away from us."

"I do assure you; her death brought me as much pain as it did yourself." I say as I remove my hood and look up to his hazel eyes. The glass wall I see behind his eyes shatters as the metal of his sword clatters to the ground.

"Alexis?" His voice is a broken whisper and he falls to his knees.

I smile and feel my eyes warm, "Hello Xander. It's nice to be able to speak to you again."

Robin clears his throat, "Alright men, Little John will attend to our guest, let us go celebrate our winnings for today." Our crew slowly files out and Robin calls to me before leaving, "He can stay for the night, but he needs to leave in the morning." I nod in understanding and wait for him to leave.

Xander just stares at me as if seeing a spector and hoping that his eyes see true.

"Xander...I apologize for my absence and the turmoil it has caused, but know that I did it to serve a higher purpose." He just continues to stare in disbelief, so I stand up and hold out my hand to help him off the ground as well; but he just moves his eyes to stare at my outstretched hand. "Get up Xander." I command. I need him to move so I know I haven't broken the man. Xander stands slowly and just keeps his eyes on me. The look of him not blinking in case I disappear is heartbreaking. I grab his hand to reassure my corporeal form is indeed real. "I did visit when I could." I say defensively. "I left anonymous citizen letters to my brother and father; and even have interacted with you a few times." His left eye twitches and I now know he is listening. "About a month after my death I saw you moping around on duty so I slapped you really hard on your back to try and break you out of your daydreaming." Xander blinks, "A few days ago I sent you a note that Ella handed to you." I pause but Xander stays silent and in shock. "You know you should talk to the other knights about upping security. It has been way too easy to sneak in and out of the castle." I scold in jest.

"Alexis... You're alive." His eyebrows are almost knitted together and his breath is uneven.

"Yes Xander I'm alive, I'm so very sorr-" He embrasses me in a hug that nearly shatters me, holding me like I am the only anchor keeping his feet on the ground. I hug him back, "I've missed you Xander." His hold tightens further and I'm having trouble breathing in the most glorious way possible.

After a few long moments he finally releases me but makes sure to keep holding my hand; I can see a thousand questions cross his face. "Tremaine is much worse than I had thought and I found a better way to help than from his side where I would have not been able to do what I have accomplished in the last four years."

That gets his attention. "How could you put us through the pain we have suffered?" He nearly drops his hand from mine but reaffirms his hold.

"You weren't the only ones to suffer Xander and with my death I've been able to help hundreds of people in the Tremaine Kingdom; ones who would have suffered more than what we had thought they would."

"I... I have to tell your family."

"No!" I command.

"But-"

"You swore on your oath as a knight not to speak a word of what you found or heard here and I expect you to keep it."

"Since you are alive, I did not fight the one to kill you so the deal is void."

"No." I state firmly, "To the world I died four years ago and that is the truth."

"Alexis you are not dead." He says raising his other hand to caress my cheek. "You are right here in front of me and you have no idea how much joy that brings me."

"Princess Alexis Belladonna Charming is dead." I state coldly. "I am no longer a princess and I do not expect you to treat me as one from this moment forward. Here I am known as Little John."

Xander shakes his head, "You must tell your family that you are alive Alexis. You have no idea what they have gone through after losing you!" Xander's hand leaves my cheek, he has never raised his voice to me before.

"I do know what I did to them and I try to relieve that sorrow as much as I can, as often as I can."

"You might have tried your best to help us with our grief, but you do not see the lasting effects!" He shouts, "Your father does not smile unless in the presence of Princess Ella or Prince Alex and even then I see it is forced." He states, "Your brother never leaves his office unless he has other business to attend to and due to this, Queen Lillian and his children are left neglected of his presence. And I-" He stops unable to force any words he has past his chest, but then wills those same words out. "I lost my best friend; not only just in a way that I could never have her the way I wanted, but that I would forever be denied to even look into her eyes or see her smile. To be told that I would never hear your voice or your exasperated sigh when men don't listen to you. That is what you did to us, that is the pain you have left us with."

There is a lump in my throat and I give a grimacing smile. "I saw and still see all of those things Xander."

"Yet you still hide from us!"

"Yes! Because believe it or not there are those who have it much worse Xander! The citizens of the Tremaine Kingdom are more like slaves that pay their master. If you saw the horrors I had seen these past four years..." I break.

"There are other ways Alexis." Xander tries to console me.

I shove him away, "No there is not! I've been in that castle and know everything that he does, has done, or is going to do. He has all the cards and announcing that he has broken the treaty will do nothing but hurt the other kingdoms!" I stop and compose myself, "Robin and his band of men are the only ones making a difference and delaying King Damian's plans. We know what our next several steps will be and if things go according to plan the Tremaine name will not last much longer."

I can see Xander does not agree with what I am saying and we stand in warring silence, he sighs, "If your plan succeeds, will you reveal yourself?"

I look into his eyes and see his plea, "I will tell only those who would most benefit from knowing. However... I will not take back my crown or title."

He doesn't enjoy my answer but seems to make peace with it for now. "When do you set your plan in motion?"

"We leave tomorrow night."

"Let me help." He says sternly.

"No Xander, anyone who works for the other kingdoms can not help. If they do they risk breaking the treaty."

"No one will know I work for the Charming family if I change clothing."

I shake my head, "You are so close with my family you are practically a part of it. Many would recognise you Xander, especially Damian." Xander's eyes falter, "He has an entire file on you and everyone close to me, he did great research before asking for my hand." He shakes his head in persistence that he will not leave and I smile, "You can wait here tomorrow night, that's the best you will get Xander."

He sighs looking at his surroundings, "Fine I will wait here."

Chapter 8

"Why has he not left? I gave you till morning." Robin says in irritation.

"Keep your knickers on, he only wishes to wait till we get back."

Robin glares at me.

"Give the man a break," Louvel chimes in mockingly, "he has just learned his lost love is alive and would like to make sure it stays that way."

I punch Louvel's arm in warning that his words are not amusing; but in truth I am merely embarrassed that he can read the situation so clearly. Although Xander and I never put our close bond into words and never acted on our feelings; it was unspoken but obvious what we had felt for one another. I shake my thoughts from my head, "Are the men ready? Were they able to purchase the tools we need?"

"Yes, are you ready?"

I nod.

"Good let's head out!" Robin calls.

We all set out on horseback Robin leads a large group of our men to the village while Louvel and I take four others to the castle. One by one we sneak into escape tunnels below and I hand out Tremiane guard uniforms to each of them; I have been collecting them for a little over a year now. Finding creative ways to steal uniforms without causing anyone to go on alert is a skill I've honed since the age of 7, finding something in my size was difficult to find though.

Once everyone is dressed, I lead our small troupe through the castle, being sure to take the less guarded halls; when we finally reach the vault there are two guards that block our path.

"State your purpose." The guard on the left commands.

"We wish to rob King Tremaine." I state bluntly and before they can comprehend my answer two of our men knock the guards unconscious. "We must hurry, take all that you can carry." I say throwing sacks to each of them as we enter the vault. "There is an escape tunnel under the rug when we are finished." I say lifting the rug and unlocking the hatch which reveals a staircase leading down to the tunnels we had entered from. We don't get far in filling the sacks before an alarm bell is sounding off.

"Thieves!"

"Out! Now!" I command.

The men all start to descend the staircase but Louvel pauses, "Come Little John, let's go."

I shake my head, "I'll find another way, just make sure the money gets to camp."

"Wait what do yo-"

"I will distract them, the money is more important, Louvel. Now go!" I slam the hatch shut locking him into the other side. Trying to keep a level head I turn to the bookcase and pull on the statuette that opens the other secret door behind. A group of guards enters the room as the bookcase closes and I break the mechanism so they can't follow, no one in this castle can know we use their escape tunnels or they will start putting guards on duty down there. I race up the stairs and feel around in the darkness for the lever that opens to the other side; once I escape the crawl space, I look to the left and a thud of pain spirals throughout my head and my vision blurs then goes black.

Chapter 9

    I awake with my head splitting, I go to hold my head in comfort and feel the weight of manacles on my wrists. It is then that I remember that I had not made it out of the castle. My eyes open and I will them to focus but I only see a shadowed figure sitting on the bench across from me. The shadow chuckles darkly, "You know," says the man I had run from four years ago, "I never truly accepted your death, I thought for sure your family or that male guard dog you call a friend had helped you escape me; but not even the best actors can mimic the scene of grief I had seen on your family's faces. I know when a light has been snuffed out of someone's eyes." Fear starts to inch through my extremities as he pauses and the light of the moon brings light to his body and a growing cheshire cat smile greets me, "Now, knowing that you have been part of the bandits that have plagued the my kingdom these last several years, I know it was your choice. Such a selfish choice would only come from a stubborn princess such as yourself."

"Selfish?" I question, I push the fear and panic down; finding strength. "I've been returning what you unfairly steal from your subjects, an enterprise of greed you have created in order to flaunt your pride."

"You could've done that from my side... and legally might I add." His eyes glint in the rising moon light.

"I would have had no power without giving away some in return."

"Now who is being too prideful." Damian stands and walks over to me pinching a strand of hair that came loose from my ponytail, "Your hair always did catch my attention." He drops the strand of hair to brush his hand down my cheek, "And those eyes so full of strength and spirit that I would take so much pleasure in breaking." He says in yearning. I try to bite his hand but he pulls away quickly and leers down at me, "Yes. Breaking you will be so much fun." His voice heavy and a sickness in his eyes that raises bile into my throat.

I spit in his face and a swift backhand pierces and then warms my face, there is a faint ringing in my ear and my headache starts to pound. "Yes breaking you will be so much fun."

"Damian!" I hear a woman's voice call from far away.

The gleam in his eyes fade as he rolls his eyes, "Because of your so-called death I had to marry that old incessant twit that you call a cousin." He stands to leave, "Now I'll give you time to think about the situation you are in because I'm going to want to know where your adorable little hideout is and you will tell me, but for now I need to attend to business. Apparently I was robbed last night."

The heavy iron door slams closed and I immediately look around my cell, I'm definitely in the dungeon, and my manacles attach to chains bolted to the wall. I tug at my restraints to test their strength and tightness; and it would seem he doesn't underestimate me. Good to know.

"Pardon me miss, but are you one of Robin's companions?" The voice is of a young man.

I look around and notice a good size break in the wall that leaks to the cell beside me. "Yes, do you know a way out of the chains?"

"No. I sadly do not, but if they come to break you out then they will help us as well won't they?"

"What's your name boy?"

"Danny mam."

"My name is Little John and I promise to do what I can to break you out. May I ask what menial law you broke to end up in here?"

"I stole some bread to feed my young siblings; my father was...recruited a few weeks ago; I'm the only one they can rely on now."

"Recruited?" I ask.

"Yes one can be recruited to work for the king in turn for a tax reduction to the family they come from, as it so happens the tax break doesn't last very long."

So Damian had started recruiting villagers already. It would seem he is using them to slowly take over villages in the bordering continent. The actual kingdom of the bordering continent is far from the border; Damian's plan is to take as much as he can quietly, then use his army when the fight really begins. It would seem we need to stop him sooner rather than later.

I sigh, "We will save who we can, and I promise to try and bring your father back as well Danny."

"Thank you princes- I mean your majest- I mean Little John."

I smile, "Please keep those titles to yourself, it has never been one I took pride in."

"Yes mam. Sorry mam. I recognized you when they dragged you in; I was younger and so excited when I heard you would be marrying our new crowned prince a few years ago. It had given my family hope that things would get better."

"Well I apologize for not following through."

"Queen Marian is great too though," he rushes to say, "she is kind when she is able to visit the village."

"She visits the village?"

"Yes she dresses like a castle maid, though she dresses that way we all recognise her easily."

I smile and let out a soft laugh, Marian dressed as a castle maid; it would seem I did rub off on her a little. "I still apologize for the years before Marian became queen; those few years could have been easier if I had followed through with my duty as a princess." My mind goes to the citizens our bandit group couldn't save, maybe I could have saved them if I'd just married him; I could have done what Marian does fo-

"No no mam, what Robin and his merry men do for us is much appreciated; I'm happy to know that the short one of the group was you princess. We as villagers were a little nervous that maybe Robin and his men might have been the cause of your death. My heart goes out to you and your family milady."

"Thank you. When we get out my existence must stay quiet. Do you understand?"

"Yes mam."

I spoke with Danny most of the day, and an extravagant meal was delivered to my cell, I fed what I could to Danny on the other side.

"May I ask why they call you Little John mam?"

I laugh, "Because I wanted to go by John but our group already had a man by that name."

He chuckles, but it turns to a cough. "Why John?"

"It's the name of the knight I used to steal uniforms and training armor from in the Charming palace."

"You used to train before joining Robin?"

"Yes, my family wasn't thrilled but I wished to be an equal with those who rule."

"I hope to be like you, will you help me train so I can join the band of merry men too?"

"I would be honored Danny."

We talk for most of the day and I'm about to lay down to get some shut eye when my cell door slams open, "Congratulations my dear. You and I are going on a little trip."

Chapter 10

I am shoved into a carriage in the dead of night, I make sure to take up the whole bench of one side so Damian can't sit close to me.

"Damian where are you going so late in the night?" My ears perk up when I hear my cousin's voice.

"It would seem I have some business to take care of."

"Now?" I take a peek through the curtained window and see that she is trying to steal a peek of who he just shoved into the carriage. She can not see me, but knows someone is in here. I quickly raise my tied hands and pluck one of the feathers I keep braided in my hair; I scoot to the other side of the bench and let it fall from my hand to the ground below.

"Yes. Now." He says frustrated with her insistence.

"Can I come with you?"

"I'll be back tomorrow or the day after. Now go to bed." He commands coldly.

Her smile falters only a fraction, "Alright safe travels dear."

Damian enters the carriage and once we start to move I look out the window behind him seeing Marian gather the feather from the ground and smirk in our direction.

"What do you have to smile about?" He huffs.

I didn't realise I had smiled and respond quickly, "I think it's hilarious you think I'm just going to show you where our hideout is."

He leans forward placing a hand on my knee, "I have ways to make you talk dear and I'll take great pleasure in using such methods whether or not you give me the information I want to know."

Fear holds me in a vice until he leans back releasing my leg. I fight back what remains of my fear, knowing I'll be able to get away from him no matter what. He will not touch me ever again.

"They call your leader Robin Hood, he was scrawnier than I pictured." He states, pulling me out of my escape plans.

"When did you see him?" I ask, because Robin is not someone I would describe as small. Although he is average height, he is noticeably muscular.

"This past festival, he won the archery tournament." He states his tone bored. "I was hoping to finally see his face but it would seem nobody but the little Charming brat was privy to his appearance; exceptional archer though."

I try to eat the smile and laugh that wants to escape.

"The only description I got from her was pretty eyes." He lets out a large sigh.

As we reach the main road, his eyes go from looking out the window to focusing his attention on me. "No questions about how your cousin is doing? From what I was told you were close even with the rather large age difference."

"Marian can handle herself." I say flatly. I already know she is okay, she is a wonderful actress after all. From the looks of it she has a lot of fun annoying this kingdom's royalty and is doing a great job of it.

*   *   *

Robin and I didn't find out about the wedding until only a few days before the event was to take place. We snuck into the castle in guard uniforms and entered her chambers once the castle grew quiet.

We took off our helmets, made sure our masks were on securely and that my hood hid my hair; and Robin made sure to cover the scar on his hand. I gently woke her, her eyes grew wide in fear but I gestured for her not to scream. I looked to Robin but he was unusually silent. Louvel ended up speaking for us.

"We are not here to hurt you Marian." Louvel says in his most soothing voice.

"Why are you here then?"

"We want to know why you are marrying him? We are part of a rebellious group in the Tremaine Kingdom, nobody volunteers to come to this kingdom much less marry its ruler...plus my boss knows you well enough and doesn't think you would agree to the marriage without a good reason."

"My cousin was coming here to help the Tremaine citizens and try to fix the problems she had found with the trade route. I was hoping to fulfill her dream of helping this kingdom become what it was when the Ferrand family ruled." I could never forget the sorrow that crossed her face. Robin visibly stiffened and had stopped from taking her hand to console her.

"Would you be willing to work with us?" Robin finally asks, but he obscures his voice.

She looked to Robin, who quickly drew his hood lower, and stood to back away when she started to look closer. "How could I help you?"

"If you see something we can help with, just pass a note along. If you know when the bursar is to collect extra taxes on the people or if you hear anything of recruitment."

We hear footsteps coming down the hall, "Yes, I'll help anyway I can."

Robin points us to the carpet at the end of the bed and then turns back to Marian, "I wish you would not have agreed to this marriage. You can always back out if you choose, we have our ways to get information from the castle."

"I lost the love of my life years ago and one of my closest friends nearly three years ago, marrying Damian Tremaine won't be the most horrifying thing that has happened in my life."

Before turning and leaving Robin lifts her hand and places a kiss to her empty ring finger.

We later established a system where she would place flowers in her window and we would respond with the feathers we used to alert one another.

*　　　　*　　　　*

"May I ask what drove you to fake your own death? I really never took you for one to inflict pain like that to her family."

"Does my choice perplex you King Tremaine?" I ask tartly.

"Just an odd choice. You could have done so much from my side and you would have lived in comfort doing so."

"The royal life never suited me and I've always challenged those who had ideals of what a woman should be."

"The fire I saw in your eyes while being scolded for dirtying your dress is what first drew me to you. My mother at the time told me to choose someone else, her distaste for your mother was no secret."

I look up to meet his eyes.

"However, I knew that you would either be a fierce woman to stand by my side, a fun toy to break, or a little of both." He leers and a shiver runs down my spine. "But you chose to die instead, forcing my plans to be put on hold."

I feel a prideful smile twitch on my face.

"Are you willing to divulge how much you know about my upcoming plans?"

"Just that you are using your citizens in your upcoming expansion." I lie.

"Mere pawns my dear."

We sit in silence for a few moments before I speak. "There are those who start a chess match with a pawn and those who start with their knight. You believe that pawns are expendable on the basis that there are so many in comparison to the other pieces. I see them as something to use as a last resort; pawns hold more power than the others because they have potential to become stronger and aid in the victory of their kingdom."

"Great rulers must use everything at their disposal to make sure they do not bend to another's will, great rulers must make great sacrifices to win the game."

"As a king, the act of playing chess means you have already lost; because what great ruler would sacrifice everything just to save, or further himself." I pause and smile maliciously, "In addition it amazes me how you treat your so called pawns knowing how strong they truly are, you of all people should know how easy it is for a mere pawn to rise in power."

Silence fills the carriage and Damian's glaring at me.

"Why would you need to use your subjects in your war anyway? You have plenty of soldiers and can call on other kingdoms to help."

"Why would I ask my future enemies for help? Enlarging my kingdom so I may break the treaty is in my favor, and I can't do it with my soldiers. Looks better if it's just a citizen skirmish don't you agree? And as for my subjects, I am recruiting them; they are volunteering of their own free will. They sign up readily to protect their kingdom and the lives they have built here. No one is being forced against their will to fight in my war." He says with a cocky smirk.

The carriage comes to a stop and Damian grabs my arm forcing me out of the carriage. He motions an arm dramatically into the dark forest, "After you milady."

I arch a brow, "You can't be serious? Why would I show you the way to our hideout?"

A sword comes swinging and stops short of my neck, but I don't flinch. Instead I look to the guard and Damian says maliciously "Either the bandit hideout burns to the ground or you and I go back in the carriage to have some fun. Although I do want to keep you to myself, you have caused me enough problems over the years that I have no qualms letting my men have some turns when I'm done." He replies.

I sigh, then I see a white feather fall behind the guards helmet, "Okay." I start walking forward whistling, signaling my fellow bandits that I will be taking the cliff back to camp.

As we near the cliff Damian raises a dagger to my throat, "Where are you taking us?"

"Whatever do you mean your majesty?" I ask coyly and keep walking, his dagger drops.

"You don't hold your life as highly as you do others, why would you take us to the hideout only because I threatened you."

"I don't know what you mean, this is the most exciting way to camp." I say as we break the tree line. I turn my head enough for Damian to see the smile on my smug face, "But you are correct I hold others lives above my own." With that I run and jump off the cliff to the river below.

"Alexis!"

Chapter 11

Swimming with one's hands tied together is very difficult. I maneuver through the raging rapids kicking my legs and using the odd boulder to catch my breath; relief is in my sights when the river calms and I see the shore line.

"You really gave your lover boy a heart attack. Took five men to keep him quiet and from jumping in after you." Louvel teases as I trudge through the water to shore.

I look around only seeing Robin and Louvel, "Where is Xander now then?" I ask as they help free me from the ropes that bind my hands together.

Robin and Louvel look to each other and nod both answering in unison, "He's sleeping."

I chuckle, "He is going to be pissed at whoever knocked him out when he wakes up."

"Yeah especially with the way we left him." Louvel says heartilly.

I turn an amused confused face to Robin. "He's tied to a tree not too far from the road, you should probably be there when he wakes up."

"Okay, what's the status of Damian?"

"He is unsure if you lived from your dive off of the cliff. There are two guards checking along the river." Louvel informs.

"Got it. I'll be on the lookout on my way to see Xander."

"Alexis? Are you okay?" Robin asks as I start walking towards the road. He raises his hand to my cheek and lightly touches my raw wrists.

I sigh, "Yes Robin I'm fine, if you guys hadn't angered him things would have happened very differently. Thank you."

Robin and Louvel nod and then break away towards camp as I make my way to where Xander is tied up.

When I find him, he is awake but doesn't see me yet because I'm coming from behind him. "I'm gonna kill that Louvel guy when I get out of these ropes." He threatens aloud.

"I'd prefer if you didn't kill one of my close friends if you can help it." I say as I cut the ropes.

"Alexis?" He lets the ropes fall and quickly turns, pulling me into his arms. "I nearly thought I lost you again."

I hug him and pat his back, "I wish you wouldn't worry so much. Are you angry?"

His hold tightens, "I can't lose you again Alexis, please stop these reckless actions that stop my heart from beating."

I sigh, "We are almost done Xander..." I pause, "Can you do me a favor?"

Xander lets me go, stares in my eyes, and nods.

"I need you to go tell my brother that Damian is about to make his next move, tell him its a message from Marian."

"Will you stay out of trouble until I get back?"

"I won't promise, but we do not have any plans to make a move against him for a few days, plenty of time for you to go and come back."

Xander rests his forehead on mine, "I'll go as fast as I can."

"I know you will. Oh, can you do me one more favor?" I take a few pieces of gold out and give them to Xander, "Can you get Alex a wood sword? I promised him a present and I'm not allowed to visit again until told otherwise."

"Why can you not visit?"

"Well someone missed a target at the festival on purpose so I would win and was almost unmasked in front of many who think I'm dead." I sass.

"I'll get him something." Xander says rolling his eyes. He encompasses me in a big hug before turning down the road, "I'll be back in four days or so, that will be my next day off."

Chapter 12

"What is our next move Robin?" questions one of our bandit brothers as I walk into camp.

"It would seem Damian will be making his next move and we must prepare with whatever we have. I know we didn't accomplish all that we had set out to do; but our plans have not changed." He replies.

I walk up to Robin and whisper in his ear, "I might have someone who knows where the first attack will be, I'm going to town to find out more." Robin nods and I grab my horse.

As I make my way to the village I notice a bouquet of red roses in a little girl's hands, and an arrow tied to them. "Little one, who gave you those flowers?"

"A pretty lady asked me to put them next to

the flag over there." She answers pointing to the wall a few yards away.

I smile, "Well I'm the person those are for, you can run home and give those flowers to your mother if you would like."

Her face lights up, "Thank you miss," she yells as she scampers off.

I look to the castle, this is Marian's alarm for something big happening. I feel as if I have no time to go back to camp, so I ride to the castle, Xander's plea for me to stay out of danger fills my head and guilt fills my chest. It's daylight but I am able to sneak into the tunnels below and put on my disguise.

As soon as I near the throne room I hear Damian's voice. "What was I supposed to do Father, everyone thinks she's dead?"

"You don't put her in the dungeon!" a booming voice shouts. "Who else knows?"

"Myself and several guards I took to find the bandit camp."

"I've heard enough of this group of thieves, you have let them get away with too much over the years. If you are not going to do what needs to be done, I'll do it for you! Tonight those bandits and their hideout burns to the ground, I don't care if the whole forest goes down with them!" The door I stand next to is slammed open as Damian's father stomps out of it, he turns to me. "You!"

A guard who was passing by and I take to an attentive stance.

"Go round up two dozen of my son's guards and those who own hunting dogs, we leave within the hour to take down the bandit camp."

I salute and turn to walk towards the training grounds. The guard that was given the same orders speaks and I try to find a way out. I see Marian, she goes to pass by me and I fall in line behind her but a hand grabs my arm, "Where are you going soldier?" The man commands. Marian turns and I look at her, I have no way of getting to one of my feathers.

"It's alright, I motioned him to follow me." Marian says.

"Lord Tremaine gave strict orders for us to-"

"This young man is part of my personal guard, there are plenty of others to choose from."

The guard takes an attentive stance, "Yes, Your Majesty. I do apologize for my ignorance."

Marian nods and smiles as the soldier lets go of my arm and leaves Marian and I to walk away, she walks to her chambers. She takes a look around to be sure nobody else is around and then pulls me into her chambers with her. "What were you thinking?!"

I cower and throw my voice, "I'm sorry, I saw your warning signal and needed to find out what it was. I need to go back to camp to warn them." I look to the armour that I know has a secret passage behind it, I begin toward it but her hand grabs my arm to stop me.

She looks at me with her head cocked, "So you are the woman that works with Robin and his men? I've never approved of him letting a lady join his band of thieves."

Her comment makes me pause, "I joined them for a reason and I can take care of myself."

She chuckles, "That's what Robin said. He sounded as if his pride was a bit wounded, you must have been able to prove yourself well. You've proven very helpful to Robin and myself, may I ask your name?"

"Among them I go by Little John, Your Majesty."

"Little John? Why take a man's name? Surely a woman strong enough to hold her own with such a rowdy group of men can choose a lady's name."

"I have my reasons Your Majesty. I wish we could speak more but I must hurry back to camp milady." I pull my arm from her grasp gently. "I do thank you for the flowers to warn us. You might have just saved our lives."

She shakes her head, "Alright, go warn them." I nod and shift the wardrobe revealing my way of escape. "Be careful dear." She adds as I step down the first few steps of the staircase.

It takes me longer than it should to take off the armor and sneak back to my horse. I can hear the soldiers and Lord Tremaine ready to set out.

My horse and I fly down the path to the dark forest; I can hear the dogs and men behind me and my already racing heart starts to pound even harder. When I reach the hideout, I shout, "Their coming! Pick up a weapon there is no time to run!"

Robin comes out of his tent and looks at me, "How are they going to find us?" It's then everyone hears the barking and howling; they quickly arm themselves.

I go to turn and try to distract the oncoming forces, but an arrow whistles past my shoulder. I turn my horse and ride towards our unwelcome guests, my horse tramples through a few enemies and as I turn to make another round I pull my feet up so that I am crouching on the saddle, once close enough I spring off and land with my blade in a soldier's neck. I look around and see that our men are keeping up. I run forward helping my fellow brethren. Arms take ahold of me from behind, holding me in place as another knight comes at me. I lift my legs and kick my oncoming attacker away before falling backwards; the man holding me loses his grip so I take advantage jumping to my feet. When I turn to make minced meat of my next opponent I see Robin in a gruesome fight with the retired king. Robin doesn't look too good and it is then that I see his blade pierce the king's heart, many must have seen it because soldiers start dropping like flies, we are surely gaining the upper hand.

Louvel startles me by taking out a soldier about to swing at me, I look up at him and smile "Thanks."

"Don't get to cocky kid, stay on guard." We both run back into battle.

Not too long after Lord Tremaine goes down, many of the guards are dropping down in surrender and we start to celebrate our victory when I see a soldier sneaking away.

I take chase, but the man gets to his horse before I can catch him; I persist by taking one of the other horses waiting for their fallen rider. I see the soldier head for the road, taking the long way back to the castle, so I take the paths I know inside the forest. As I ride towards the castle I feel a cold wet drop hit my face, a moment later a few more fall and before I know it the rain is pouring down. I don't have time to change into a Tremaine uniform so I opt for sneaking in under the cover of this dark rainy night. I'm able to use the tunnels to get to the kitchen, no one is working inside so I wait for the guards nearby to pass before I sneak past the entry way across. There are stairs that lead to the dias that sits above and opposite the royal throne; on the dias are doors that lead to an outside balcony giving me a perfect place to wait for the runaway messenger. I hide in the shadows with an arrow at the ready for the soldier who is to bring news of the fight to King Damian Tremaine. I get my breathing stable and I calm my nerves; it is only the bow and arrow waiting for the incoming target.

"You have nerve my dear," comes a malicious whisper to my ear. Suddenly I am in the air and then pain shoots from my shoulder to my hip, all along my right side. Air has left my lungs and I am on the ground outside the throne room; I attempt to catch my breath as I look up to see Damian jump from the balcony landing on the ground a few feet away from me. I put a leg under me to stand and achieve it with little grace due to the pain engulfing my entire right side; I quickly take out a dagger that is holstered to my leg and take my best defensive stance; Damian unsheathes his sword.

"Your leader took my father's life." He says as he makes his first attack, I spin out of the way and nausea spikes from the pain of doing so. How did the guard get news to him before I could take him out?

"Yes, well it is only fitting since he was the one to take the man's family from him." I slash at Damian but he takes a step back dodging my attack. He looks confused. "It would seem your father didn't make sure everyone died before taking the throne." I shrug my good shoulder, "Not checking up on royal deaths must run in the family." I taunt him.

Damian's face ticks and he growls, "The Ferrand prince is still alive?" He spits to his left, "I'll be sure to correct that mistake!" He yells as he goes for another powerful swing, I dodge, but my speed is slower to accommodate my injury and his sword slices at my bad shoulder. I want to scream out in pain but refuse to give him the satisfaction. He leers and that familiar shiver runs down my spine, "Come dear, I'm going to make you scream one way or another and trust me this will be much less scarring." He starts to swing at me in succession and all I can do is counter. After a few more hits I see my opening, I counter his swing and then hold my breath to swing my right arm to strike him in the liver. He keels over slightly and I back away letting out a painful breath as a torturous throb radiates from my fist through my arm and to my injured side. He has regained his composure and comes back to strike at me again, but his swing is too high so I take my chance slamming my blade upward into his chest. My calloused hands are bloody from the force of his strikes so I can't tell until he slumps onto the ground that I hit my mark. He gasps for air and holds his chest. He looks to me and smiles, "You were right about one thing."

I give him a confused and sorrowful look as I place my arm around myself trying to bring comfort to whatever is bruised or cracked from the fall. "What is that?"

He hisses a laugh. "You really don't live up to your family name."

I walk over and place my boot to his wound making him cough and whimper. "How was I brought down by a mere girl playing with a sword? It would seem my mother was the only one to kill a royal and get away with it." He chokes out in anger but then smiles at me, "She killed your mother you know?"

Shock barrels through me, "My mother died of sickness." I protest.

"My mother poisoned her," he announces laughing but it transitions to a heaving cough. "She always hated Queen Ella, always went on and on about how she stole Prince Charming from her. Thankfully she met my father who was ambitious enough to take the Ferrand Kingdom, but she didn't seem happy until word of your mother's death spread throughout the kingdom. When she died a few years later, I had found out what she had done after reading her journal. I can't say I was saddened by the revelation; your mother made sure not to let my family near you or your brother. I was only able to approach you after her passing; I don't believe your father knew who my mother even was."

Anger starts to slowly seep into every fiber of my being, nausea threatens to take over.

"I was so close to fulfilling our goals, my family could have ruled over all these puny kingdoms and expanded out into the continent."

I give a small grin and pull my hood on, "Your plans would have never worked, because you, nor your father know how to truly rule a good kingdom. You see only weakness in our treaty and not the strength behind it. As I have ascribed before; you let greed and pride blind you."

He huffs out a pained but sarcastic laugh, "If only you had married me, things could have been so different."

I smile down at him maliciously, "Oh you are wrong if you believe that was your downfall." His smile fades and his eyes grow hooded; I pick up his sword from the ground. "Your biggest mistake was seeking me out in the first place," I say as I swing the sword down, finishing him off.

Chapter 13

As I stare down at the man whose life was just ended by my hand, I don't notice the soldiers who have come in and now hold their swords to me. I wait unmoving, keeping Damian's sword in my hand, I refuse to yield to these men if I must fight them I will.

Marian's voice comes from behind me, "What is going on-" she gasps.

"An intruder has killed King Tremaine, what shall we do, Your Majesty?"

"Drop your weapons." She says bluntly as if these guards should know better. "May I ask your name?"

The Tremaine name is gone. My mind races as I look down once again to Damian's lifeless body; the citizens are saved...I can go home, I can see my family and be with Xander...I... I killed someone. That thought overtakes me, I don't feel like the same person anymore. That had always been so important to me, not changing; it is what I have revolted against in all of my years as a princess and a bandit. But now I've killed someone and I did it in anger; I didn't need to kill him. He could of-

"Pardon me, your name? I promise you no harm." Marian's voice brings me back.

I turn to her, and the realization of being able to reveal myself and go back to my family hits me hard. I'm not the same person, but I did make a promise. "My name is one you know well." I say not altering my voice.

"You are the woman from the bandit group. Robin was right in that you are very capable."

Some pride swells in my chest.

"I do apologize," she says with some discomfort twitching on her face, "But I don't wish to call you Little John, may I have your real name miss."

She can see only darkness from my hood and mask. I reach up and untie the mask and then take down my hood as well, "It's so nice to speak to you again dear cousin."

Marian falls to her knees, her hand comes to her mouth and tears start to spill down her face. I hobble over and try to kneel down to her level but my side resists, "I'm injured so I need you to come up here."

She shoots up and encases me in a tight hold and immediately gentles when I suck in air due to the spasm that runs through me.

"You're alive." She says in disbelief.

"Yes, I'm alive... and I'm wearing ugly masculine clothing too." I say trying to humor her.

She pulls away laughing, her eyes sparkle, "It is the most beautiful outfit I have ever seen you wear."

I smile and we embrace each other once again.

Chapter 14

Marian had my injuries tended too and she immediately readied several horses so we could ride to the Charming Kingdom; I've been advised not to ride but I told the doctor just to give me medicine for the pain. When we get to the forest I part from the riding party to go update Robin and the others.

"Robin?! Louvel?!" I call.

"Alexis! Thank goodness you're okay." Robin calls from behind me. He wears a bandage over one eye and a sling holding his arm.

"Did we lose anybody?"

"Not yet. There were a few men who have some pretty bad injuries, but we have already sent for the doctor." Louvel says, he only has a few scratches on him, he looks to my hips, "Your hurt as well, what happened?"

Robin sees how I'm holding myself on my horse and gives me an anxious look.

"Damian is dead." I blurt out.

Many eyes in the camp go wide as heads whip in our direction.

"Are you sure?" Robin asks.

I let out a huff of laughter, "Since I was the one to deal the final blow, yes I'm sure." I feel guilt start to creep in and my eyes start to burn but I reign it all back.

"How did you get out of the palace without being seen?" Louvel asks.

I start to eat at my bottom lip and look away from my two friends.

"Alexis?" Robin asks in a warning tone.

"Marian and a few soldiers are aware of who I am, they are on the road not too far from here, we are on our way to my kingdom-" Robin breaks out in a sprint toward the road. I look back to Louvel, "There is a general waiting for some of us to go bring back the citizens Damian sent to fight; would you mind taking a few men to meet with him?"

Louvel nods, "I'm very proud of you little one. I'm sorry you had to take a life; even if he was a bad person. Let me know if you need to talk about it, taking a life can weigh on a person."

I nod and Louvel turns to the men, gathering a party to go meet the general.

I ride back to Marian and the other Tremaine knights. When I get to them, Robin is nowhere to be seen, he must have already talked to Marian, who seems to be holding back a smile. "Let's go greet my family." I say and start down the road, word getting out about me being alive will spread like wildfire; I want to be the one to tell them. As we ride, the numbing agent the doctor had applied starts to wear off but I persist. We reach the kingdom border and I tell Marian I'll meet her in the throne room.

"Why are you not coming with me?" she asks.

I force a smile on my face, "I don't want others to know before they do."

She gives me an unconvinced glare but lets it go.

As she and her guards ride toward the castle, I choose to walk to the tunnel entrances. I dismount my horse and grab my side that is burning, a string of curses mumble out of me as I hiss at the pain. It is excruciating to put the armor on, shots of pain run up and down my side when I lift my arm or bend over. I made sure to pull out the poltase that the doctor gave me for pain and reapplied, the torment is nearly blinding me and stars seem to dance in front of my blurring vision. I wait for it to take effect before going to the exit nearest to the throne room, I curse the stairs feeling some prickling climbing them. When I get to the door at the top I take a few deep breaths and then put my helmet on.

I exit and walk slowly to enter the throne room. When I enter everyone turns to look at me, Marian isn't here yet.

"Is something wrong soldier?" My brother asks.

I then realise how unsteady I must look, I try to straighten but my side is unwilling to let me. I'm about to fall when someone catches me and I realise it's Xander. He makes sure that I am steady on my feet and I raise my left arm and slap him on the back, wincing a little at the vibration that makes it to my right side. I can see a second of anger but then realisation shoots through him. Xander smiles and turns to lock me in his arms, he gentles his hold when I stiffen and let out a small hiss.

"Xander?" My brother's voice sounds very confused and I let out a small huff of laughter, only loud enough for Xander to hear.

He backs away, "Are you okay?" He asks and starts checking me and I nearly lose it at how odd this must look to my family. Xander goes to raise my right arm and I quickly pull away wincing and let out another hiss. He looks as if he can feel my pain, "Your hurt. Who did this? I'll-"

"Don't worry he's already taken care of." I whisper.

I hear a small gasp and then little feet slapping the floor. My niece and nephew stop in front of me, Ella smiles and points to my chest and then I see that Ella's bow she had given me is not tucked into my helmet. Her and Alex look up to me all smiles, "Have you come to tell us more stories?" Ella asks excitedly.

"Thank you for the gift." Alex says politely.

I pat their heads.

"We have been wondering who tells them stories of Queen Ella and Princess Alexis." My father says as he walks over to me, he stays a good distance away but I can see him clearly. "It is wonderful to know that a person so loyal to our family could regale them with stories that pains us too much to remember."

"She's really pretty too!" They both clamor in unison.

"She?" I hear my brother and father question.

"Yeah her hair looks like daddys but long and pretty!" Princess Ella claims and then gasps.

The twins look up to me apologetically, "It's okay little ones," I say smiling as I remove my helmet, "you can tell them all about me now."

The room is silent and the look on my family's faces... My father steps forward slowly, tears on the brink of falling down his face. He lifts his hands to my cheeks and I lean into his touch. He pulls me forward and wraps me in a tight hug, I need to lean on one side to alleviate the pain and I hug him back, "I'm so sorry."

He pulls back shaking his head, "Sorry?"

"I know how much pain I caused by my actions and I'm sorry."

He shakes his head, "You are here, there is no need for apologies."

I look over his shoulder to see Lillian coaxing my brother out of his shocked state and I start to hobble towards him; Xander quickly comes to my side and helps me walk more steadily. I smile at my brother, "Hello brother, you did such a great job all these years. I do hope you will let me take over some of your trade route plans so you will spend time with your family more. I hear you haven't been living up to your duties as a husband and father, did those tutors teach you nothing?"

Tybalt takes hold of my hands and dips his forehead to mine, his eyes are shut tightly bringing harsh lines to his face, "You will never understand the immense happiness your presence brings to this family and our kingdom. It's been so difficult without you Alexis."

"You're our Auntie Alexis?" My nephew asks.

"Yes, I was off on an important mission, but its over and I can come home now."

"What have you been doing all these years?" Tybalt questions.

"True to form, I've been getting into mischief, causing havoc, and not acting the way a lady or a princess should." I sass, I begin to laugh but a shot of pain shoots from my hip and I step away into Xander's careful hold.

"Alright, you really need to have another doctor take a look at her!" Marian scolds loudly from the doorway, startling all of us out of our happy bubble.

I chuckle when everyone starts fussing, they had forgotten about my pained state in the shock of learning I was still alive.

Xander carries me to my old bed chamber and lies me down on the bed. He, Tybalt, and my father leave only when the doctor comes to look at me. Apparently my riding had made my injuries worse.

Once the doctor left telling the men I needed to stay in bed to rest until he takes another look tomorrow night, Marian snuck inside to lay with me.

She lays there smiling, "I'm so happy to see you again, I was a mess when I had heard. To lose my love and then my closest family; it broke me Alexis."

I give her a sympathetic smile, "I was always there when I could be."

Her smile grows, "Yes I know that now. Robin came more than you did, but I always knew when you came too."

"I mostly snooped at night, Robin was the brave one to come during the day."

I turn and see a large smile on her face and longing in her eyes. It is then I realise that she still referred to him as Robin.

"He proposed to me, you know." She states, shocking me further.

"Really? When?" I ask, when the hell did he have time for that?

"When I separated from you. I saw a feather and told the guards I needed a break to compose myself before meeting with my family; it is why I was late. I went into the trees and after looking around I turned to see him on one knee."

I let out a small huff of humorous air, the cocky bastard didn't even wait till she buried her previous husband; although we all know it wasn't a real marriage. "What was your answer?" I ask curiously.

"I said yes." She whispers. "I feel uneasy though, I feel that I'm betraying Erec."

The man didn't tell her? What the hell is he waiting for? Was 17 years not long enough? I sigh, "I'm sure he is okay with your decision Marian, thrilled even."

"Am I crazy to accept when I have never even seen his face?"

I shake my head, trying so hard not to burst into laughter, "Trust me the man is up to your standards in every way."

She looks at me and smiles. We lay in silence and I am only vaguely aware when she sits up and leaves for her guest quarters.

*   *   *

I wake to a dip in the bed beside me, when I open my eyes I turn to see Xander sitting on the edge with his back to me but his hand rests atop mine. I smirk up at him, "You know, it isn't proper for a man to enter a ladies chambers without supervision?"

His shoulders shake in laughter as he turns towards me with an amused grin gracing his face, how I've missed those dimples. Such an easy smile that takes me back to when I first started to understand my feelings for him. His gorgeous hazel eyes are alight with so much happiness and love, I can do nothing but mirror him.

"Xander?"

He lifts and places a kiss on my bruised knuckles, "Yes, my princess."

I give him a glare but then give a small chuckle and beam up at him, "Will you marry me?" The blank look he gives me says that he doesn't believe he heard me correctly. "Xander?"

"I truly am eternally and irrevocably in love with you Alexis." He states with a watery smile, "You are a woman who refuses to act as her gender is told to act, takes pride in doing so, and therefore is beautiful because of it."

I look into his eyes, "I love you too Xander." He then leans down and places a soft kiss upon my lips. I smile, "Can I take your answer as a yes?" I ask.

He chuckles and pulls out a small ring that looks like leafy vines encircling each other; he places it on my finger, "I've had that ring in the pouch you gave me for nearly six years now." I look up from the ring confused, he smiles and shrugs, "I always lost my nerve; something I really hated myself for all these years."

I smile and go to one of the braids in my hair pulling a simple silver band from it. "I've had this for the last three years. I saved a young woman from being hung for a crime she did not commit; her father was a black smith and gave me this ring as a thank you for saving her." I place the ring on his finger; and we both stare at one another smiling. "Thank you for waiting Xander."

Chapter 15

It has been several days and the kingdoms have decided to meet to decide who is to take over rule of the Tremaine Kingdom. The group of bandits have also received invitation and I had fought my family to be able to walk with them; I had won the argument obviously and now stand near the entrance with Robin, Louvel, and my fellow comrades.

"Mind telling me why you still hide your face from Marian?" I question Robin. He turns and his eye twitch in a glare. We all wear our hoods and masks more out of condition than need. I hadn't shown my face to anyone in four years and the rest of my brethren have been hiding for years longer, some even more than a decade.

Louvel looks smug as well.

"I wish to finish with this first before revealing myself."

I turn to Louvel, "You know he proposed to her?"

Louvel lets out a hearty laugh and slaps Robin on the back, "Congratulations."

Robin glares at me again but I shrug and turn to enter the building, our group following behind.

We stand on the ground below the royalty looking down from their dias'.

"We welcome the man by the name Robin Hood and his merry men. May I ask which of you was the one to kill King Tremaine?" asks King White.

I step forward and bow, "That would be me Your Majesty and I would love to extend my congratulations to your newest addition to your family."

Queen White holds her baby daughter closer to her chest, the queen is paler than I remember her, she was always so kind to my family. "We would like to know your reasoning for causing the Tremaine Kingdom so much trouble as well as killing your king." She interjects gracefully.

"I must be truthful that I was never a citizen of the Tremaine Kingdom and I can only speak for the time I had truly known the motives of King Tremaine; but he had plans to expand and then take over the rest of your kingdoms as well. I had killed him only in protection of my own life; although I take little sorrow in taking his life. His downfall was pinnacle to my family's safety as well as all of your kingdoms in the first place."

"May we ask your meaning? You sound as if he came after you first young lady."

"You would be correct Queen White. Damian Tremaine came after me first, and I thank these men behind me for giving me shelter and allowing me to help with their cause all these years. To them I am Little John, but to many of you" I take my mask and hood off, "many of you knew me as Princess Alexis of the Charming Kingdom." There are many hushed whispers and gasps, "I do apologize for my absence, but the truth was that the treaty all of our family's had signed many years ago had blinded us to King Tremaine's tainted motives, had he not threatened my family and myself. No one would have been able to stop his plans before it was too late." I say firmly.

The room becomes loud with arguments and protests of my involvement with the death of King Tremaine.

"You weren't kidding about not being all that graceful politically," Louvel whispers in amusement.

I turn to him, "Never had lived up to my name or my gender."

Robin sighs and all the men bark out in laughter, which silences most of the court; they seem horrified that the men are laughing at such an inappropriate time.

My brother stands to address the room, "Before we speak of the problems of the treaty and the fact that my sister has potentially broken it; I believe that crowning a new king to the now vacant kingdom takes precedence. We all know that the citizens have been treated poorly all these years, they deserve better."

Everyone seems to agree and King Swan speaks up first, "Seeing as Alexis was the one to slay the king we must ask if you would like to nominate anyone from your group of bandits?"

I nod, "I would like to nominate Queen Marian Tremaine and her new fiance." I say boldly. Some begin to speak but I cut them off, "It is no secret that you would all be sceptical of my choice, but I feel that there would be no better ruler than the woman who has been protecting all of you in her own way and the man," I pause and point to Robin who stiffens, "who was set to rule the kingdom before the Tremaine's took it for themselves."

Confusion hits everyone's faces, but I hear a single gasp from the Tremaine side. Robin steps forward and starts to unmask and take his hood off, "May I present Erec Ferrand, son of King Arthur, previous first prince of the Ferrand Kingdom."

The room becomes noisy with chatter once again. My father steps down to the ground floor where we stand and stops in front of Erec he looks into his eyes and smiles. Marian comes out of nowhere and tackles Erec to the ground. You would think she was me for a moment seeing as Marian is the picture of being a lady.

"Are all in agreement of her nomination?" My brother asks.

All are in agreement and the motion passes that first prince Erec Ferrand will be crowned in the coming weeks, for now Queen Marian is to hold power in the proceedings. It takes nearly all day however everyone has come to an agreement on a new treaty, which now includes expanding our trade routes and a meeting to revisit the treaty every five years.

* * *

The next few months are a blur, Erec Ferrand is now king with his wife Marian at his side. I am now Lady Alexis Nikolaidis; although it took some hard headedness to get my family to agree, I renounced my title as princess; I was never suited for the role anyway.

Xander and I live in the palace, and I now help him train new recruits; my brother also put me in charge of our new ocean trade route. I took the position without question, my brother needs to spend time with his family; I have taken a role as one of his advisors as well.

I have chosen to keep the truth surrounding my mother's death to myself, there was no need to tell my family and bring them unnecessary pain.

Xander and Louvel have been helping me with the guilt I feel; killing someone, no matter who it is, takes its toll.

I had alluded to happy endings being a joke and although I believe happily ever afters are not what you should aim towards; I believe happiness, no matter the road it takes to get there or how long it lasts, should be cherished for every moment in life it fills.

The End

www.ingramcontent.com/pod-product-compliance
Lightning Source LLC
Chambersburg PA
CBHW070757120626
46557CB00002B/640